The Walk Back Home

Kizzie Le Carpentier

Illustrated by Victoria Starskaia

The Walk Back Home

Copyright © 2020 Kizzie Le Carpentier

ACKNOWLEDGEMENTS

I'd like to thank Kat Broadhurst for her work
on this book as editor and proofreader,
and to Mary Rusthel Sarmiento for doing the
layout design and format.

CONTENTS

INTRODUCTION

I wrote *The Walk Back Home* for a university assignment in my first year as an undergraduate (2018). It's a short story about a 5-year-old girl named Sam who is trying to find her way back home. On the way, she meets a cat namcd Oreo, a soldier called Luke, and a deer with no name. They all decide to accompany her on her journey.

The story concludes with them arriving at Sam's house and observing her family through a window. There's a framed photo of Sam with a candle next to it. These symbolically seem to suggest that Sam is, in fact, no longer alive.

The theme and message of the story are simultaneously shown through humour and melancholy, demonstrating the notion that although Sam's life has ended, her adventure still continues.

The story's concluding plot twist is not only unexpected and striking, but it also provides a potential educational talking-point. Because of the nature of the story's ending, there is the prospect of further sequels that can continue with Sam's tale.

CHAPTER 1, THE CAT

To the rhythm of small strides, she marched ever onward through a thick horde of snow, as thick and full as giant clumps of wool. Her little legs marched forward.

Like a soldier, she thought. Like a muscle-man; a muscle man in pink army armour with glittery boots, and a feathered hat!

The snow began to pummel down. The cold, icy wind tugged at her blonde curls and heavy pink coat. As the wind swirled, she pulled the coat's hood over her to protect her eyes. It was too late for her nose; the cold had caught it ages ago. Once again, she readjusted her scarf around her neck, pulling it up over the lower part of her face. She tried in vain to quickly brush off the excess snow that kept sticking to her blue jeans and coat.

Is it this way? She glanced all around her.

Looking ahead, she could just about make out two paths to choose from. The one on the right was thorny, bushy and crawling with trees—trees that looked like their branches could grab, snatch and pull at you until something scary, like a wolf, was at your heels.

I'll go left, she thought. It seemed like the most obvious choice.

The left side was clearer to look at. You could almost make out a road in the middle of the rows of trees that lined either side of it. The snow lay thick, as though the ground was being used by the clouds as a dumping ground for the bin loads of snowflakes pouring down, gradually getting heavier and heavier.

"I need to find some shelter," she decided, picking up the pace as she jogged along her chosen path. Her pink wellie-boots crunched on dead leaves and twigs as she pressed forward.

Up ahead, she could see an old wooden bus shelter. She dashed towards it, running against the wind that seemed so determined to stop her.

"You'll not get me!" she yelled at the ferocious blasts of air. "I'm no mere Kid—I'm Sam!" She then let out a mighty "RAAARR!"

Clenching her fists, Sam charged her way through the gusts and made her way past the pine trees. She focused on the shelter until finally, she got to it. With one last burst of energy, she threw herself forward, clung to the shelter's wooden beams, and pulled herself inside.

Staggering forward like a drunken sailor, Sam tripped slightly and stumbled to the bench. Heaving with all her might, she lifted herself up and perched on the hard seat. Sitting cross-legged, she took a deep breath…

"What's a small fry like you doing all the way out here?" she heard a voice remark.

Sam frantically looked around her for a moment until she spotted a shadowy black figure under the bench. It crawled out, jumped up onto the seat and looked up at her. Sam stared for a short time into the creature's eyes. They were yellowish-green, with large black pupils.

"A cat?" she asked in a whisper.

"Yes, I am a cat. I haven't seen a person for a long time," said the cat. His tone of voice was mellow but seemed somewhat rough and under-used.

"My name is Oreo," continued the cat, softening his eyes as he continued to look at the girl. "That's what my owners called me. What's your name, small one?"

The cat then sat up in a princely manner and waited for Sam's answer.

"Sam," she replied quietly. "How can I understand you?"

Oreo replied, "Here, it's different. In this place, we can speak freely to one another and understand each other."

The cat turned his head in the direction of the storm and looked out, staring thoughtfully ahead. The wind was starting to dwindle, the angry howl halting to a soft whistle.

"I'm trying to find my way home. I'm lost," said Sam to Oreo, as warm slivers of water dribbled from her eyes and onto the bench.

"Now, now, there's no need to cry," soothed Oreo. "I'll help you the best I can. What does your home look like?"

CHAPTER 2, THE SOLDIER

The pair eventually left the shelter and walked for a little while. The sun had finally decided to show its face, shining through a small space between the grey clouds. The once ominous and dark path now looked like a winter wonderland. Sam could see the trees, topped with what looked like white icing. The wind was no longer noticeable, and there was the fresh smell of nature which comes after a storm.

"It's so pretty!" Sam squealed in delight. She excitedly shook her hands around in a frantic attempt to get rid of all her pent-up energy and nerves.

"EEEEEEEE!" Sam shouted gleefully as she ran ahead, hearing the crunch of the snow as it flattened beneath her boots, her trouser legs brushing together in an ungraceful manner.

"Careful of the ice!" shouted Oreo from behind her.

Sam craned her neck back to look at Oreo and skidded to a stop. Feeling her legs give way to a slippery patch of compressed snow, she collapsed to the floor, bashing her head and elbow against the cold hard ground. Sam made a whelp-like sound, like that of an injured little puppy. She rolled around on the floor for a short time, before sitting herself up again.

"Are you—" Before Oreo could finish his question, they both heard the loud shout of a man.

"ARE YOU OKAY?"

To their right, a man came sprinting down the small road that connected to theirs. His heavy footsteps boomed as he hurried towards them.

Sam could see a huge man with short shaggy hair, just visible from under his green hat. Thick stubble was on his chin. He was wearing a green army suit and had on a giant pair of commando boots—the reason why his steps made so much noise.

She sat on the ground, watching the stranger canter towards them.

When he was a few away feet from them, the man started doing a ridiculous type of dance. He waved his arms crazily in the air while making odd out-of-control leg movements. It all looked very silly to Sam.

The man rapidly started to pick up speed. He whizzed right past them and smacked straight into a tree…

He had slipped on some ice.

Oreo and Sam stared at the man. He was still for a moment, awkwardly arched over next to the tree with his bottom in the air. The man slowly sat himself up, looking dazed and sheepish.

Eventually recovering himself, he got back up on his feet. He then walked towards Sam, knelt down and offered out his hand.

"Are you alright? You took a nasty fall there!" he said, looking at her with kind eyes.

"Pfft!" replied Sam, trying not to giggle. "Am I okay? Are you okay?!"

Oreo was now next to Sam, eyeing the man with a cautious look on his face. Once again, he sat down beside Sam like he was nobility.

"Yes, that was quite a fall," Oreo said as he stared at the man in green. "Who are you?" he asked, impatiently waiting for a response.

"Oh, that? That was nothing—just a little trip. Nothing more!" the man replied. He pulled Sam up onto her feet and brushed off the snow from her coat. He didn't let go until he knew that she was steady on her feet.

"Talking animals…They're a bit…a bit…unorthodox," said the man, looking down at Oreo wide-eyed yet unimpressed by a talking cat.

Oreo's expression changed from impatience to that of annoyance. His tail twitched slightly.

The man looked back at Sam and gave a warm smile; it reminded her of her dad's.

"My name's Luke. Where are you heading to all by yourself?" He looked down at Sam with concerned puppy-like eyes, ignoring Oreo who was by her side.

Sam could see the twitch in Oreo's tail quicken.

"I'm Sam. I'm not alone, though; Oreo's taking me back home," she said gently stroking the cat.

"You're lost! If you'd like, I can help get you home. A cat is not much protection. I, on the other hand, was in the military for 20 years." Luke seemed determined.

Now proudly standing up straight, with his chest out and his hands on his hips, Luke declared, "I'll accompany you home. What do you say?"

Oreo's tail was now flicking back and forth at a steady yet ferocious pace.

CHAPTER 3, THE DEER

"Hey, ho! Away we go!
Donkey riding, donkey riding!"

The still, tranquil surroundings made Sam and Luke's singing echo. The three new companions were walking on a much bigger road now; doubled-sided and very wide. Signs were positioned on both sides, with arrows pointing in different directions. Salt was scattered everywhere, making the snow turn brown. Everything indicated that this piece of road was still in use.

"Hey, ho! Away we go!
Riding on a donkey.
Were you ever off the Horn
Where it's always fine and warm?
Seeing the lion and unicorn
Riding on a donkey!"

Sam and Luke bellowed out their little tune, creating an unhealthy amount of noise for just two people. Luke was looking down at the road as he walked with Sam on his shoulders. Taking several large steps at a time, Luke patrolled forward. He looked back at Oreo.

"Are you keeping up, Cat?" Luke called out.

"Yes. No need for your concern!" replied an irritated Oreo. He looked up at Luke, narrowing his eyes as though he'd been deeply offended by the man's question. "And for the record, the name's Oreo, not Cat!"

The three came up to a bend in the road, which made it impossible to see beyond it. It felt as though they'd just gone around in a giant circle, but they carried on. As the road started to straighten up again, a shape in the distance made the group stop in their tracks.

"What's that?!" Sam called out.

"A deer," said Luke swiftly and calmly.

They walked a few dozen steps forward until they were a foot away from the animal. Sure enough, a small deer stood on the left side of the road. It was looking directly ahead and was utterly oblivious to the trio behind it.

"Hello!" Sam said, greeting the animal.

Startled, the deer leapt backwards. It then ran forward a little before coming to a halt. It turned around and just stared at them for a long time, dragging out a comedic silence before opening its mouth to speak.

"No. No further. Stay back." The deer had a quiver in its voice, and its legs were shaking tensely. Its large eyes stared wildly at them.

"It's okay, we're not going to hurt you," reassured Sam, sliding off of Luke's shoulders and plonking to the ground.

"Careful there, Sam, he's already spooked enough. Deer are feeble creatures," Luke advised her in a firm tone.

"Feeble?! They're terrifying!" called out Oreo. The cat had caught up and was staring coldly at the deer. "Please don't bring this one with us, Sam!" he begged.

"Huh? Bring me with you? With you where? Where are you going?" The deer replied so suddenly and unexpectedly that it made them pause in surprise.

After a short pause, Sam explained, "I'm going home."

"Home? What's a home?" asked the deer, intrigued. It was still being cautious and keeping its distance.

"A home is a place where you spend time with your family," smiled Sam as she answered.

"Like a field? Is your home a field?" the deer asked with inquiring eyes.

Sam looked at the deer, and her smile grew even broader, "No, but it has a garden, which is kind of like a field."

"A garden…Like a field," murmured the deer. A soft noise like a sigh escaped from its large nostrils. "I'll come with you. But keep your distance."

Luke looked at Oreo's unimpressed expression with an amused look on his face and let out a quiet chuckle.

CHAPTER 4, HER CANDLE

With Oreo taking the lead, the group continued towards their destination. Soon Sam came across a familiar sight.

Ahead was a scratched white wooden gate in the middle of a sturdy fence which encircled a vast garden. Peach, pear and plum trees—shrivelled and leafless in the winter cold—were dotted all around the
terrace. Tall pine trees, still green and proud in the winter air, engulfed the surrounding area.

A white house stood in the centre of the garden. It had four big wooden framed windows. To the side of the house was a garage with a distinctive old, red, 5-seater car inside. The house blended in well with its surroundings; white snow littered the ground and treetops as it had done everywhere else.

Directly in front of the gate, leading up to a big ash door, was a grey stoned path that had recently been swept clear of snow. Oreo, who had taken back his spot at the head of the group, stopped and sat down by the gate, waiting for Sam.

Seeing the house, Sam's footsteps became slow, and she started to shuffle forward.

"Is this the right place?" Oreo asked, looking directly into Sam's eyes, a stifling sadness starting to take over him as he reads her emotions.

"Yes..." she answered very quietly.

"How did you know of this place?" Luke asked Oreo, staring directly towards the house.

"I've been past this house lots of times," Oreo said modestly, his head turning to follow Luke's gaze. "It's not far from mine. When Sam described her home to me, this place came to mind."

"Wow. Well, good job, Oreo," replied Luke.

Oreo looked up at Luke, astonished at this unexpected compliment.

"A box? A box with a field around it…" Looking around in wonder, the deer gave the house a nod of approval. Amused at the deer's reaction, Sam, Luke and Oreo chuckled to one another.

"You need a name, we can't just keep calling you 'deer'," Luke said, looking at him.

"I thought Deer was my name!" Deer exclaimed.

Luke took off his cap, rubbed his forehead, put the hat back on, walked up to Sam and put his hands on her shoulders.

"Go on ahead, we'll be right behind you." He gave her a gentle push forward.

Taking a deep breath, Sam outstretched her right arm and opened the gate. She walked straight in and down the long, stoned path to the window to the left. Oreo, Luke, and the deer followed closely behind her. A bench was positioned perfectly underneath the window.

With one swift motion, Luke lifted Sam up and placed her onto the windowsill.

Through the window, Sam could see the living room, seasonally decorated with tinsel, coloured fairy lights, and dazzling ornaments. Figurines of Father Christmas and his reindeer were on the mantelpiece, directly above a roaring fireplace. A fluffy beige carpet stretched out and claimed every section of the floor. A giant Christmas tree stood in the far corner; an 8-foot tree covered in beautiful, shiny stuff.

Sam's eyes darted towards the big red sofa, a couple of paces away from the fireplace, where three people were sat.

She saw her mother, her blonde hair matching her own. Her father was sat next to her, his beard looking even more impressive than Luke's. And then there was her new baby sister, dressed up in Sam's old pink fluffy dressing gown. It had been Sam's favourite when she was that age.

They were sat close to each other, with her sister on her mother's lap. The three looked happy, reading a book together, cuddling up like little penguins huddled together.

Sam looked back at her new friends and smiled faintly before continuing to look through the window. Her gaze fell on something—a photo of herself on the side table next to the sofa. The photo had been taken at school; she was wearing her plump pink coat over her uniform, and her hair was up in a neat ponytail. The picture was in a golden frame. In front of it was her single lit candle, burning brightly.

Printed in Great Britain
by Amazon